Jessica Souhami

KING POM

and the Fox

F

FRANCES LINCOLN
CHILDREN'S BOOKS

There was a man called Li Ming
who owned nothing but a pomegranate tree.
  He looked so proud guarding it that people laughed
and called him "King of the Pomegranate Tree"
or even just "King Pom"!

One day, some of his precious pomegranates
were stolen, which made Li Ming so angry
that he set a trap to catch the thief.

He poured a jug of sticky gum around the tree,
hid in the shadows, and waited.

Very soon, a red shape slunk by the tree,
reached for the fruit – and stuck fast
in the gooey mess.

It was a big red fox.

He looked at Li Ming coolly.

"Don't just stand there, King Pom," he said.

"Get me out of here and I'll make you rich!"

"Well," shrugged Li Ming, "I've nothing to lose."

And he pulled the fox out of the gum.

"Thanks!" grinned the fox.

"Now promise to do as I say.

Ask no questions.

Show no surprise.

Leave everything up to me."

Li Ming promised.

And the next morning they set out.

The fox led Li Ming to the river bank near the Emperor's palace.

"Take off your clothes, King Pom," he said, "and jump in the river. Remember! Ask no questions. Show no surprise. Do exactly as I say!"

So Li Ming undressed and slipped into the freezing water, just as some courtiers from the palace were passing by.

"HELP!" shouted the fox. "My master, King Pom, is drowning!"

The men pulled the shivering Li Ming from the water
and the fox continued.

"My master was on his way to the Emperor," he said,
"carrying priceless gifts of gold and jewels, when a huge band
of fierce robbers attacked him, threw him in the river
and took everything. Even his horse and clothes."

What a smooth-tongued liar of a fox!

The courtiers gave Li Ming fine clothes to wear
and took him to the Emperor.

Li Ming and the fox received a warm welcome.

"Pity about the stolen gifts," mused the Emperor. "But what a fine young man. And so rich! King Pom would make an excellent husband for my daughter."

And the princess was thinking the very same thing.

And so was Li Ming.

And so was the fox.

But the Prime Minister was suspicious.

"Let me escort you home, King Pom," he sneered. "I'm longing to see your splendid palace."

"My palace?" thought Li Ming. "How will the fox get me out of this?"

So the Prime Minister, Li Ming and the fox set out.

Before long, the fox saw in the distance
a caravan of camels laden with rich silks and jewels.

He raced ahead to greet the herdsmen.

"I've come to warn you," he said. "Those 'gentlemen'
are in fact wicked bandits. They'll rob and kill you,
unless ..." and the fox grinned, "... unless you say
these are King Pom's camels. Then you may pass in peace!"

And, sure enough, as the caravan passed, the herdsmen
called out, "Make way! King Pom's camels coming by!"
Li Ming was amazed.
The Prime Minister was impressed.
What a cunning rogue of a fox!

Very soon, the fox caught sight of a distant troop
of magnificent horses. He dashed ahead to meet the grooms.

"I've come to warn you," he said. "Those 'gentlemen' are
in fact wicked bandits. They'll rob and kill you, unless ..."
and the fox smiled, "... unless you say these are King Pom's horses.
Then you may pass in peace!"

And, sure enough, as the caravan troop passed,
the grooms called out, "Make way!
King Pom's horses coming by!"
    Li Ming was astonished.
    The Prime Minister was pleased.
    What a sly rascal of a fox!

As dusk fell, they came to a splendid palace.

The fox ran ahead and knocked at the door.

The palace belonged to an ogre, and he opened the door.

"WHAT DO YOU WANT?" he bellowed.

"Well," said the fox. "I've heard you can change into any animal you like. And I don't believe it!"

"OH, DON'T YOU?" shouted the ogre. "JUST WATCH!"

And he turned into the biggest, fiercest tiger in the world!
   The fox was terrified, but he just said,
"Oh, a BIG animal is easy. I bet you can't turn into
a little creature – like a bug."

With a **ROAR**,
the ogre turned into a tiny green bug.

The fox squashed it flat –
and that was the end of the ogre!

So when the Prime Minister and Li Ming arrived
the fox was ready to welcome them to
'King Pom's magnificent palace'.

Li Ming was relieved.

The Prime Minister was satisfied.

What a brave and daring fox!

They returned to the Emperor
and the Prime Minister told him all about
King Pom's wealth, fine possessions
and the magnificence of his palace.

So Li Ming and the princess were married
and lived happily ever after ...

... and the fox lived in luxury
all the rest of his days.